Karen Lee Schmidt

Carl's Nose

Harcourt, Inc.

Orlando   Austin   New York

San Diego   Toronto   London

Requests for permission to make copies of any part of the work should be
mailed to the following address: Permissions Department, Harcourt, Inc.,
6277 Sea Harbor Drive, Orlando, Florida 32887-6777.

www.HarcourtBooks.com

Library of Congress Cataloging-in-Publication Data
Schmidt, Karen.
Carl's nose/Karen Schmidt.
p.   cm.
Summary: Carl the weather dog, famous for his accurate prediction of
bad weather, has to find a new sense of purpose when the climate in his
mountain town of Grimsville changes from storms to sunshine.
[1. Dogs—Fiction.   2. Animals—Fiction.   3. Weather—Fiction.
4. Weather forecasting—Fiction.   5. Mountain life—Fiction.]   I. Title.
PZ7.S355Car   2006
[E]—dc22   2004014670
ISBN-13: 978-0-15-205049-8   ISBN-10: 0-15-205049-3

First edition
A C E G H F D B

Printed in Singapore

The illustrations in this book were done in watercolor and gouache
on Arches cold-pressed watercolor paper.
The display type was set in Olduvai.
The text type was set in Minister.
Color separations by Bright Arts Ltd., Hong Kong
Printed and bound by Tien Wah Press, Singapore
This book was printed on totally chlorine-free Stora Enso Matte paper.
Production supervision by Jane Van Gelder
Designed by Lydia D'moch

To my Carl, who has a fancy for sunshine,
and brought me fair weather
—K. L. S.

Carl had a nose for bad weather.
From the sharp smell of an ice storm
to the thick, sweet odor of a typhoon,
Carl's nose was never wrong.

Carl and his nose lived in Grimsville
at the foot of Old Man Mountain.
Every morning that mountain reached
into the sky and whipped the clouds
into a terrible fury. Those storms had
nowhere to go but down. The weather
in Grimsville was worse than bad.
It was perfectly awful.

But Carl and his nose saved the day, every day, with their accurate forecasts. Everyone at Big Marie's Cafe tuned in for "The Carl Report." In a town with not much to celebrate, Carl was a celebrity.

While Big Marie and Tiny Norman served Five-Alarm Chili, Carl waxed eloquent on clouds: "The aroma of cumulus congestus cannot compete with a whiff of nimbostratus, and neither packs the wallop of the fragrant thunderhead!"

Tiny Norman whistled a song of warmth and firesides. Carl chewed chili. *Life is sweet and good,* he thought.

But mountains are mountains and they think mighty highly of themselves. One day, Old Man Mountain took a sudden fancy to sunshine.

When Carl stepped outside to sniff for bad weather, a soft breeze caressed his face. He was so alarmed that he predicted the most terrible storm ever!

Carl mis-predicted the weather every day of that gloriously sunny week—and the next week, too.

I have a nose for bad weather in a town where there is no bad weather. That's like having no nose at all, thought Carl. These are dark days indeed.

In despair, Carl retreated to his storm cellar and lay down for a nap. When he awoke and saw the sun still shining and felt the breezes still breezing, he lay down for another nap. And so it went, nap after nap, day after day.

Then one sunny, sunny day as Carl napped, Tiny Norman wandered barefoot near the base of Old Man Mountain. Whistling songs of endless summer, he followed berry bushes deeper and deeper into the forest.

CLANG, CLANG, CLANG! The village alarm bell woke Carl.

A terrible storm? He sniffed. *Fat chance!* But still, the bell drew him to the town square.

"Help! Help!" cried Big Marie. "Tiny Norman has disappeared! I found his wee shoes under a berry bush near the mountain!"

Oh, what a big smell came from Tiny Norman's
oxfords—of spilt milk from Sunday, froggies and snails
from yesterday's wade in the creek, . . .
Suddenly, Carl's nose twitched, shivered, and sniffed
high into the air! Was that the smell of Tiny Norman?
It can't be, thought Carl. *I need a nap.*

But Carl's nose had other ideas. Tugging, sniffing, and snuffling, it began to pull him along, toward the mountain.

Carl's nose led him into the deepest forest. Imposing smells of danger surrounded him. Pungent Peril! Malodorous Risk!

Brave Carl stepped still further into the piney woods and sniffed with all his might. The scent of Tiny Norman grew stronger and stronger and stronger. Then suddenly, a sound drifted through the trees . . . a high mournful tune of being lost and alone.

Carl followed the scent and its frail melody far along the treacherous trail. Many sniffs later, down a slippery slope, he found Tiny Norman.

Carl led the little whistling wanderer back to
Grimsville. Big Marie gave Carl a hug that smelled
of chocolate.

Cheers rang through the streets. "Hurrah! Hurrah
for Carl! Hurrah for Carl's nose!"

Nowadays, Carl is much too busy for naps.
But sometimes, when Old Man Mountain
needs a cool drink and pulls a sweet little
rainstorm out of the sky, Carl does give a
weather report.